DR. ANDROMEDA FALLOUT

RAY THORNE

Dedicated to my family and friends for all
their support over the years—from my
childhood until today.
Each and every one of you is special and
holds an important place in my heart.

Allison Finkle sat in her VW Beetle and sighed. She clutched the steering wheel tightly before opening the door and getting out. As she crossed the long, empty parking lot toward the building that housed Omega, she thought about the events leading up to this moment. The moment of needing to get a job right out of university. The moment in which all her dreams of working in the field she had received her doctorate in collapsed.

The country had become a much different place than when she had left it eight years before—it had become a hard place. The government had been taken over by a fascist dictator who had crept into the system before the rest of the country could blink twice. Now everything was controlled to the point of suffocation. To men and women, freedom was but a memory.

Allison believed she could have done great things to help protect her country with her knowledge in nuclear and atomic studies and experimentation. She was on the brink of creating a device that would eliminate any nuclear or atomic blast, and now she stood in front of Omega, the only company that would pay anything someone could live on. She had heard that this place paid well but that it was a very hard work environment. That was all she knew—and that she needed to eat to live. She opened the door to the building and stepped inside.

Allison was greeted by a man dressed in a radiation suit and helmet. "You must be Allison Finkle," said the man. "We've been expecting you."

"Yes, that's me," said Allison, as chipper as possible. "I've brought my work credentials with me as asked."

"That'll be all for now," interrupted the man. "Stand up straight please, miss."

Allison arched herself up as straight as possible while the man looked up into her eyes.

"You're awfully tall, aren't you?" asked the man, rudely.

"Yes, sir," replied Allison. "I'm the black sheep of the family in that department."

"How tall are you?" asked the man.

"Six feet, six inches, sir," replied Allison.

"Well, we will have to put you on one of the larger lines, then," said the man.

"Yes, sir," said Allison.

The man ordered Allison to follow him down a hall nearby.

"Once you are briefed by our supervisor—his name is John M.—he will show you the work area in which you'll be placed," said the man.

As they walked down the hall, Allison noticed that the man was carrying an instrument that looked like an extremely sharp ax. She tried to brush it off as simply something he used for the work he did but couldn't help but get an uneasy feeling about it. They entered a small office with a young man sitting at a desk at one end of the room. An empty chair sat across from the desk.

"Please take a seat, Miss Finkle," said the man at the desk.

"Thank you, sir," said Allison. She walked across the room timidly and sat down in the empty chair.

"You may go now," said the man at the desk to the man at the door. The man at the door bowed as he left, shutting the door behind him.

The man at the desk leaned back in his chair, awkwardly looking Allison over from top to bottom. "You're a very pretty woman, Miss Finkle," he said. "I'm John M., and I will be your supervisor. What brings a woman like you into Omega? Surely you could have found other places to work for."

Allison gulped as she felt vomit well up in her throat, aghast at John M.'s comment. "I heard this is a good place to work, and I need a steady job," she stammered. "I hope I'll be a good asset to the workforce here, sir."

"Oh, you will be," said John M., winking at her.

Allison stood up in shock. "I'm sorry, sir, but I think maybe I am not the right fit for Omega," she said sternly, trembling with disgust.

"Why the sudden change of heart, Miss Finkle?" asked John M. slyly. "After all, you just said you needed the job."

"I think I'd better go now, sir. Thank you for your time," replied Allison. She turned to leave.

"But you can't leave now," snarled John M., angered by her casual rejection of what he had hinted at. "You already signed your work contract before your first day, which is today. It's against the law to leave the site without permission."

"Against the law?" asked Allison, perplexed.

"Yes, miss," said John M. "You don't want to go to jail for breaking the law under code section 517, which has been in effect for the past three years now. Were you living under a rock or something?"

"No, sir," replied Allison. "I was in school in another country, studying abroad for the past eight years."

"Well, you have a thing or two to learn now that you're home," said John M. coldly. "And here at Omega, you'll learn the ropes in no time."

Allison felt her insides drop to the floor. "Yes, sir," she whimpered.

"Now follow me," said John M., motioning her toward the door.

They walked down another hall that led to the main factory floor. The workplace was large, with many lines running multiple parts used to make nuclear explosives. A massive nuclear reactor towered over one end of the plant, letting out an eerie hum that over time could deafen one. To Allison's puzzlement, she noticed quite a few workers with robotic prosthetic limbs working here and there. The limbs appeared to move on their own, doing the work, while the workers themselves seemed to be exhausted and downcast.

"Now get into your work uniform, Miss Finkle," said John M. A small young woman with robotic legs walked up to greet them. "This is Mia," continued John M. "She will show you where to change."

Allison smiled at Mia. Mia nervously smiled back, looking up into Allison's caring eyes.

"Please come with me, miss," said Mia timidly. She guided Allison off the floor and into a locker room, where they walked up to a locker with a bench in front of it and sat down.

"This will be your locker, miss," said Mia.

"Please, call me Allison," said Allison. "The formal forms of address used here aren't my thing. It's not very personal."

"There's nothing personal about this place," said Mia suddenly, looking down at her legs.

Allison looked at Mia as she stood up to open the locker. She began to change into her uniform.

"These work uniforms look like prison garb," said Allison.

Mia slowly nodded in response.

"If you don't mind me asking, what happened to your legs?" asked Allison as she sat back down next to Mia.

"I had to go to the bathroom too many times one day," replied Mia.

"What?" asked Allison, shocked.

"That's what they do to you here," continued Mia, looking down at her legs. "If you don't stick to the guidelines here at Omega, they're permitted to do what they call 'corrections.' If your limbs cause you to not perform the way the company wants you to, they replace them with their own manufactured ones. It was that time of the month for me, and I ended up needing to use the restroom more often than what's allowed. It resulted in my needing corrections."

"They can do that?" exclaimed Allison.

"It's the law," said Mia, tears welling up in her tired eyes. "There is nothing any of us can do about it. It's life now."

Allison, wide-eyed, leaned back against the locker and put her hand to her forehead. She swept her hair off her face and took a deep breath. "Okay," she said. "I'll do my best."

"There's no best here at Omega," said Mia, standing up, her legs clanking on the ground.

"There is only better, and if you don't succeed, they'll make you try and try until your death, if it comes to it."

Allison looked down at Mia and nodded in understanding.

"I've said too much, by the way," Mia said quickly. "Please don't say anything to John M. You seem like a good person, Allison."

"What makes you say that?" asked Allison.

"Your eyes told me," replied Mia quietly. "Everyone here's eyes are dead or blank. You know what I mean? The life is gone from them. Once I saw yours, I knew you were special."

Allison smiled, but her lips trembled. She didn't know what to feel as terror gripped her heart, so she followed Mia back out onto the factory floor.

As they arrived at the section of the work line in which they were to work, Mia began to brief Allison on how to do the job. They were putting together the final assembly pieces for what looked like a large metal capsule.

"What are these parts we're making?" asked Allison as she carefully connected wires to their respective terminals.

"They're bombs," replied Mia bluntly.

Allison knew this but wanted to be sure since they were set up differently than the ones she had learned about in her studies. She questioned the safety, in her head, of the wiring harnesses used for production. "These will corrode in no less than a year," she said to herself. "Not a good safety feature at all."

"They're used within a month after being made," said Mia abruptly.

Allison looked up at the girl, shocked. "What?" she said quietly to Mia. "This is enough explosive to demolish a ten-story building!"

"Our country's leader has been keeping many of the other nations at bay as well as preventing any of them from traveling to outer space. Many want to just leave Earth now," said Mia.

"I knew we were at war with a lot of them, but not to the point of churning out this many bombs in a single day," continued Allison. "Is much of what we're doing top secret or something?"

"Very much so," replied Mia. "However, things are in such a state in our country that no one even cares, just so long as we do what our leader says."

Allison looked down in disgust at the part she was working on. She knew what she was doing went against her moral code. After all her work in the field of neutralizing bomb damage, she was now building them with her bare hands.

Suddenly a fist slammed down on the table next to the two women. "Enough chitchat! Get back to work!" shouted a man from behind a radiation mask.

"Yes, John M.," said Mia.

Allison looked up at the figure of John M., now gowned up in a radiation suit. He walked away holding one of the ax instruments Allison had seen the man she met earlier in the day carrying. She sighed, looked at Mia, then continued working.

Later that afternoon, Allison sat in the cafeteria with Mia on meal break.

"So, how long have you worked here?" Allison asked Mia as she poked the potted meat on her plate with a fork.

"Almost three years now," replied Mia.

Allison looked back down at the plate in front of her. "What did you do before working here?" she asked.

"I started here right out of high school," replied Mia. "Not much work experience at other places, but then again, there hasn't been much of a choice in today's day and age."

"Yeah, it's been rough. I was surprised when I got back to my parents' place after university," said Allison.

"How are your parents doing?" asked Mia.

"They passed away a year ago," replied Allison quietly.

"Oh, I'm so sorry," said Mia.

"Yeah, Dad passed a little before Mom did in a traffic accident, and Mom a little afterward from cancer," explained Allison. "I'm sure they're in a better place now."

"That's sad," said Mia. "That has to be hard."

"Thank you, it was, but I'm coming around," said Allison. "I was gone for quite a long time at school."

"What did you do at the university?" asked Mia.

"I got my doctorate in nuclear physics, with a specialty in nuclear and atomic radiation studies," explained Allison. "My hope was to find a way of eliminating a bomb explosion's impact on the cellular and atomic levels."

"And you wound up working here at a nuclear bomb factory," chuckled Mia, before taking a bite of her food.

"The irony of it all," mumbled Allison sarcastically.

At that moment, an elderly gentleman walked up to the table where the women sat, holding a tray of food. "May I join you ladies?" he asked politely.

"Of course! Sit down, Olin," replied Mia as the man smiled and sat down.

"Allison, this is Olin," said Mia. "He works in a different area than us."

"Nice to meet you," said Allison, shaking the man's hand.

"You're new here, aren't you?" asked Olin.

"Yes, sir, it's my first day on the job," replied Allison.

"Is Mia here teaching you the ins and outs of this joint?" asked the man.

"She sure is," replied Allison. "I'm hoping to do well in my first week."

Olin's hands began to shake as he reached for his fork. "I'm sorry, but I struggle with Parkinson's fits from time to time," he explained. "Every day, I have to watch myself on the floor so I don't cause a scene for the supervisor."

"I'm sorry to hear that," said Allison sympathetically.

"He's had a couple close calls with the ax," interjected Mia, knocking her fist against one of her legs.

Allison swallowed hard and winced at Mia and Olin. They stared back at her seriously.

"Well," started Mia, breaking the awkward silence. "It's time to go back to the floor."

"We barely had any time to eat," murmured Allison as she stood up.

"That's how it goes here. Don't want to get back to the line even a minute late," said Mia.

The two women said goodbye to Olin at the table and walked back to the factory floor.

When they arrived, both were met by hard and sudden smacks to the backs of their heads by John M. "You're thirty seconds late!" growled John M. "I know it's your first day, Miss Finkle, but Mia, you know better!"

"I'm sorry, John M.," said Mia as she looked at Allison. "It won't happen again."

John M. walked away, and Mia looked over again at Allison, who was rubbing the back of her head, a tear falling down her cheek.

"They have a metal plate in the gloves on their suits," said Mia. "That's why it hurts so bad. It'll pass, though."

Allison nodded, shivered her emotions away, and took a deep breath as she went back to work.

In the weeks that followed, Allison began to learn the work-related practices in effect at Omega. She watched as Mia struggled with her legs and winced in pain to keep from soiling herself between the minimal times they allowed her to walk off and use the bathroom. She watched Olin receive raps on the head for having shaking fits from time to time. It hurt her to see such an elderly person, or anyone for that matter, being treated that way.

"This place is horrible," said Allison to herself as she attached a wire harness to a nuclear terminal on the part in front of her. Suddenly John M.'s fist slammed into her face. The strong blow threw her onto the floor. When the fogginess left her sight, she saw blood dripping onto the cement at her feet. She put her hand to her face and realized her lip and nose were bleeding.

"Have a hostile attitude today?" asked John M. angrily as he stood above Allison, who knelt hunched over on the floor.

"I'm sorry, sir," replied Allison, standing up shakily.

"You should know by now that that kind of talk will get you into trouble, miss," hissed John M.

"Yes, sir," said Allison with no inflection as the blood dripped from her mouth. She was beginning to feel as though she was going to burst with rage at any moment, but she kept it bottled up.

"You know," said John M, "I can probably get you special treatment, get you off the floor, if you'll do something for me."

"Like what, sir?" asked Allison, feeling the burn of tears in her eyes.

"Well, like what I hinted at when you first arrived here. You could do me a personal favor, and perhaps I'll be able to get you a more comfortable position," replied John M.

Allison wanted to throw up. Was this what the world had come to? Was this what was permitted by work policies now? Was this what was permitted across the board by the government?

"No thank you, sir," said Allison coldly. "Now if you'll permit me to return to work, I am ready to do so."

John M. growled beneath his mask and clenched the ax instrument in his hand. "Very well," he responded, and walked away.

Trembling, Allison breathed a sigh of relief and sat back down next to Mia to begin work.

"Wow, you got guts!" whispered Mia. "No one has ever brushed him off like that in my whole time being here."

"Really?" asked Allison. "He is disgusting. I can't believe it's tolerated here."

"Our country's leader apparently permits things like that in the workplace. I miss the time when I was a kid and things were different. My parents basically live in hiding now," replied Mia.

As Allison nodded in agreement, shouts emanated from across the factory floor. The two women looked up toward the noise and watched as John M. stood screaming over Olin, who was shaking violently. The old man fell from his seat and onto the floor. A group began to gather as the incident unfolded.

Mia couldn't stand up, since at this time her legs did not permit her, so Allison ran over to the group. She pushed her way through the group of people to the front and watched as Olin lay shaking, with John M. yelling at him to stand back up.

"He's having a seizure or something!" exclaimed Allison.

John M. looked up at her in surprise but ran for medical help. Allison kneeled next to the man and laid him on his side.

"Get out of here," muttered Olin.

"I'll stay with you until help arrives, Olin," stammered Allison.

"No, I mean . . ." the old man continued, choking on his words, "get out of this place before they get you too."

"But how?" asked Allison quickly. "It's against the law."

"The nuclear reactor . . ." replied Olin. "Turn that thing up the next chance you get. Then get yourself and Mia out of here . . ."

Olin's eyes went dark as he breathed his last breath.

Allison, wide-eyed in horror at the now dead man beside her, stood up and stumbled her way toward Mia, who had laid her head in her hands on the table where she sat, immobilized.

"He's gone, isn't he?" whispered Mia, shaking.

"Yes, he is," replied Allison.

She looked up from Mia sobbing at the table and toward the nuclear reactor across the room. She saw the guard standing by the levers. Her eyes narrowed in on it in hatred and fear.

"Turn that thing up the next chance you get." Olin's words rang in Allison's head.

She tucked the thought into the back of her mind and sat down next to Mia.

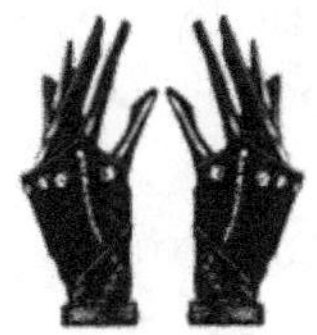

Months passed, and things didn't get better for Allison or Mia. Allison grew more and more discontented with the work she had to do as she constantly noticed mistakes were being made with the products. She tried to correct mistakes when she could but watched as the parts went out onto the loading docks.

If only people knew how unsafe this all is, Allison thought to herself. *We could all be blown to bits any second. Maybe this was Omega's goal? To create an unsafe environment on purpose for some strange reason?*

Mia, on the other hand, started to get sick. She started getting paler and paler as the days dragged on. One day she needed to get to the bathroom, and Allison noticed as she walked that her legs began to malfunction. They would randomly lose power, causing Mia to have an unsteady gait.

"I shit myself," said Mia to Allison one day as she sat down. "Sorry for the smell. I can't do this anymore. I am going to die."

"Oh, Mia!" exclaimed Allison. "Let's get you help!"

Allison waved John M. down as he walked by. "What is it?" John M. asked bluntly.

"Mia needs help," Allison explained, towering over John M. as she stood up. "She had an accident, her legs aren't working properly, and she looks as pale as a ghost."

"You did it on purpose, girl!" hissed John M. to Mia.

Mia sat silently as she closed her eyes, wincing. "I'm in so much trouble," she said to herself.

"I'll help her if you'll permit me to do so, sir," said Allison, trying not to glare at John M.

"No! We have assistants for such occasions," barked John M.

He called over his walkie-talkie for assistance, and two nasty-looking women appeared shortly afterward. They rolled their eyes and made rude comments as each slung one of Mia's arms over a shoulder and they dragged her to her feet. Allison looked into Mia's eyes; they were bloodshot and glossy, with the deepest feeling of sadness and exhaustion in them. Allison battled the hot sting of tears.

As they helped walk poor Mia away from the floor, basically dragging her since her legs appeared to have stopped working altogether, Mia looked back at Allison with a small, tired smile. She did so all the way out the door as Allison stood like a statue on the floor next to John M.

"Is she going to be okay?" Allison asked John M.

"They'll take care of her, miss," replied John M. "Although it's none of your business anyway."

Allison looked at John M. as he walked away. "Mia and I need to get out of here. Regardless of prison or whatever punishment the law allows," she said to herself as she sat back at the worktable.

As the day dragged on, Allison noticed some faulty wiring harnesses and stopped putting them together in the part to inspect the box they came from. She discovered that they were outdated. With an eye roll and a sigh, she pushed the box to the side and paused for a moment. She looked at her hands and saw the calluses and cuts all over them from the work.

That was when a wall of metal flashed across her vision, blinding her view of her hands, followed by a loud thud on the table. Allison screamed as she felt a hot painful sting shoot up her arms and down her spine. In shock, she looked back at the table and saw her hands and part of her forearms lying on the table, detached in a pool of blood. An ax instrument sat planted in the table.

Still screaming in pain and anguish, she looked up into the masked face of John M. He had cut off both her hands!

"Get a cauterizer in here!" John M. hollered over his walkie-talkie.

Allison began to grow faint from blood loss. She fell onto the ground, and as she began to see everything going into a fog, she looked at the bloody stumps that were once her hands.

"This is what happens when someone needs corrections, miss," said John M. condescendingly.

Allison watched everything go black as she passed out.

The nurse's station met Allison's eyes when she woke up. A nurse walked into the room and stood beside her.

"How are you feeling now?" asked the nurse.

"I don't know, ma'am," replied Allison.

"Once you feel like you can stand without feeling dizzy, you can get your things and take the rest of the day off," said the nurse. "Your new hands will be here tomorrow, so be here bright and early to be ready for work."

Allison sat up and moved to the side of the bed. Once the fog in her eyes settled, she looked down in terror at her arms. Bandages covered the stumps that were her forearms.

"Since you can't drive after the corrections trauma, someone will drive up shortly to take you home," said the nurse.

Allison trembled as she walked out of the nurse's station to the locker area to grab her things.

There she was met by John M., who shoved her up against the locker. She sank to the floor.

"Let this be a lesson to you, Miss Finkle!" he snarled. "I can see in your work and attitude that you refuse to comply with us here at Omega and with me as your boss! So from here on out, you need to realize that you belong to this company! You can try to run when you're out and about not working, but we will find you and bring you to justice. You'll face severe penalties for not complying with the country's leadership and laws, since you'll be found guilty of treason. Do you understand?"

"Ye-ye-yes, sir," stuttered Allison, trembling with fear.

"Now, get out for today! Your ride will be here shortly and will meet you out front. That is all," ordered John M. as he stormed out the door.

Allison rose awkwardly to her feet since her arms hurt so badly. She couldn't get a grip on anything to help herself up either. Once she painfully managed to pull her coat and purse from the locker, she walked out of the building's door and into the freezing blizzard outside. As she looked around for the driver that was to pick her up, she noticed the figure of a worker lying in a snowbank. She rushed over to the person.

It was Mia. She was covered in a fresh blanket of snow, so Allison quickly and painfully tried to rub it off the girl, who lay there motionless. "Mia! Mia! Can you hear me?" exclaimed Allison as she lifted the girl's head into the crook of her arm.

Mia slowly opened her eyes, and a glimmer of happiness crossed them.

"They got me good this time," said Mia as she struggled to force the words from her frozen lips. "My legs stopped working altogether, so they sent me home and told me to never come back."

"Why are you out here? You'll die!" exclaimed Allison.

"The driver never came, and I am too weak to move now," stammered Mia. "I got out of Omega for good, Allison . . . I . . . got . . ."

Mia's head fell limp in Allison's arms. She was dead.

Allison broke down in tears and cradled the small body lying there. "I'm going to get you back home, Mia," she said. "I'm going to get you back home to your parents. I promise."

The driver arrived to pick up Allison, so she picked up Mia's body with what little energy she had left and got them both into the vehicle. The driver looked back at Allison holding the girl in the back seat.

"I'm sorry," said the driver in a caring tone. "This isn't the first time this has happened. I'll help you get her back home."

Allison looked up at the driver, who looked back and nodded in understanding.

"She is lucky," continued the driver. "She doesn't have to be in this hellhole of a place anymore."

Allison silently agreed with the driver and leaned her head on Mia's as the vehicle disappeared into the blizzard around it.

The next morning Allison arrived early at Omega, as requested by the nurse, for her replacement hand procedure and installation. She was brought into a back room that held a small laboratory and machine shop. A man in grease-covered overalls approached her and asked her to take a seat. Allison did so while he brought out two glistening black metal hands on a cart and tray.

"Here they are, miss," said the man. "They will take some getting used to, but they'll work very well, I think."

Allison stared wide-eyed at the hands. They looked menacing. The fingers were joined with screws to the knuckles in a primitive fashion. Maybe it was their simple appearance mixed with the shiny black metal that gave Allison an uneasy feeling, but she swallowed her fear and accepted the situation.

The man injected her with a local anesthetic in both her arms to numb them, then proceeded to attach the hand-and-forearm devices. After around an hour of manipulating wires inside the hands and attaching them to a spot on her arms, Allison looked down at her new appendages.

"Okay, miss," said the man. "Now raise your right hand, please."

Allison did so slowly. It felt weird moving the fingers when she couldn't feel anything while doing so.

"Now your left hand, please," said the man.

Allison did so, with the same results.

"Now come with me, please," ordered the man, waving her into a side room.

Allison followed him into the dimly lit room, where a metal pipe and a brick sat on a table. They walked up to the table, and then the man walked over to an intercom in the corner of the room and shut it off.

"Now, Miss Finkle," said the man, "I tried something new with your particular hand model."

"What is that?" asked Allison.

"If you swear to me you won't tell anyone here at Omega, I'll explain it to you," replied the man, almost yearningly.

"What do you mean? Not tell Omega about what and why?" asked Allison.

"You were that new employee, right? The one who tried to help out Olin that day he died, right?" responded the man.

"Yes, I am," said Allison.

"Olin . . . was my father," stammered the man.

"I am so sorry," said Allison.

"My father and I have been forced to work for Omega for many years," explained the man. "We worked in the field of prosthetics and artificial intelligence before that.

We were coerced by the government to extend our services to their new work control plan here."

Allison listened intently.

"After my father began suffering from Parkinson's disease and seizure-like tremor fits, he was unable to do the detailed work here in the lab and machine shop," continued the man. "Since they couldn't let him go due to his knowledge of this place, he was sent to work on the lines."

"That is awful," lamented Allison.

"My father mentioned you to me a while back after he met you that day in the cafeteria. For some reason, he got this premonition that you don't belong in a place like this, even though you probably had no choice when you took the job," said the man.

"That is correct," agreed Allison. "I needed a steady-paying job. I just needed it to live and eat, pay bills, and possibly put it toward my experiments."

"Well, my father looked up your credentials file from the university you attended," he continued. "And needless to say, you need to get out of here—and fast. When the bigwigs find out what your knowledge level is, they either put you into higher positions or destroy you for the sake of our country's leader. John M. knows that, and he knows it well."

"Before you continue, I have one question for you, sir," said Allison.

"Yes? What's that?" asked the man.

"If you're the one who makes these appliances for the workers who undergo corrections, then why were Mia's legs permitted to die on her?" replied Allison somewhat coldly.

"It was beyond my control, miss," said the man. "They saw her as a useless employee and pulled the plug on the wireless control panel for her legs."

"So, Omega murdered her?" asked Allison.

"In a way yes, but also no, miss," replied the man. "It isn't against the law, and there's a clause about it in the employee contract. She wasn't the first, and she won't be the last."

"So, I guess, explain to me what 'new thing' you did with my hands," sighed Allison.

"Okay," started the man excitedly. "I've built yours so that they cannot be controlled by the wireless panel here at Omega. I set up a dummy one for you here in case anyone wants to check on it."

Allison's eyes began to brighten with surprise.

"Most hand appliances I make are designed to squeeze and grip things with the same power as a typical human hand," continued the man. "Come over here please." He motioned Allison over to the pipe and brick lying on the table. "Now pick up that pipe," he ordered.

Allison clumsily tried to pick it up and, after much struggling, did so awkwardly.

"Just give it some time and practice," said the man. "Now, bend that pipe."

"Bend it? It's around four inches thick from the open center!" exclaimed Allison.

"Bend the pipe," ordered the man again.

Allison took the pipe in both hands and, without much effort, bent it into a pretzel shape and crushed the metal where she gripped it as if it were tinfoil. She dropped the thing to the ground and gasped.

"Break that brick, please," said the man.

Allison picked up the brick with one hand and started to squeeze it. The man turned away from her and covered his face. The brick exploded into dust in her hand! She coughed as she dropped the remnants.

"I've given them enough strength to move or break just about anything with the power of a hydraulic press," said the man gleefully.

"That's very cool and all, if not daunting," interjected Allison. "But why did you do this for me?"

"You didn't deserve to have your hands removed," said the man. "This is my payback to you for being kind to my father when he needed it most."

"Thank you, I guess," muttered Allison, still perplexed.

"The nuclear reactor," said the man abruptly. "Remember what my father told you? The nuclear reactor."

Allison stared deep into the man's eyes in understanding. She bit her lip and looked down at the ground.

"Next week is Christmas vacation," he continued. "Most employees will be out of the building that week, and all bomb shipments will be off the docks and sent out. They don't store them in the plant when the building is closed since the place isn't safe to leave explosives like those unattended."

"Okay," said Allison as she clenched her fist angrily. "I think I get the picture."

"The danger-level meter and control lever are located where the guard stands by the nuclear reactor," he explained. "Once it's turned up into the red zone, you'll have precisely fifteen minutes to get as far away as possible. Do you understand? Have your car ready to book it once you're out of the building."

"All right," agreed Allison seriously.

"Remember," whispered the man, "never let anyone know what went on in this room today." He walked over to the corner of the room and turned the intercom back on, then showed Allison out of the room.

As Allison walked down the hallway to the main factory floor, she thought about everything the man had said to her earlier. She also thought about Mia, and tears once again began to sting her eyes. She wiped them away with the cold steel fingers of her hands and thought about all the things she wouldn't be able to do with them now. She had been playing the piano since she was a little girl, and this realization stunned her. And she wouldn't be able to do the detailed work she needed with her future experiments. "I'll get through this," she muttered to herself. "Only takes time."

As she entered the main factory floor, Allison was met by John M. He stared coldly at her. "I see you're all set and ready to go," he said, taking the handle of his ax instrument and tapping her hand.

Allison felt a surge of fear and adrenaline spike throughout her body as he did this, but she managed to maintain a calm demeanor. "Yes, sir. It might take me a while to get used to them," she said, "so I trust that I will be off the line I was on until I can finish my occupational therapy?"

"You'll sweep. I don't want to find a speck of dirt anywhere by the time you're through with it," he ordered as he walked away.

Allison sighed and grabbed a broom from the maintenance closet.

As the days continued to pass leading up to Christmas vacation, Allison managed to use her sweeping duties to get closer to and around the nuclear reactor to scope it out. She saw that the guard always carried a stun gun. She noticed that the stairwell leading up to the main deck of the reactor came up from behind the facade of the humming inferno, and that the guard stood about ten feet off to the side of the stairwell opening by the control levers. This left her with little opportunity to sneak up on the guard to disable him. This factor was the only dilemma she faced in this diabolical operation.

However, by this point Allison didn't care about the dangers. She began to feel colder and icier inside as the days passed. She alternated between thoughts of warmth and extreme sadness. Warmth to the point of thinking about childhood memories of being home with her parents on Christmas Day, and sadness to the point of death. She watched as fellow employees worked like robots, were reprimanded, then left for the day. Day in and day out. She looked over at the spot where Mia used to work, which now sat empty. *It's almost time,* Allison thought to herself. *It's almost time to end this.*

The last day of work before Christmas vacation arrived. Allison swept around the workers, keeping an eye out for when they were out of the building for the day.

In the evening, before closing, John M. walked up to Allison. "I'm going to need you to stay later and clean up the cafeteria," he ordered. "The cleaning lady is out early for the day."

Allison agreed and kept on sweeping. She knew it was a good opportunity for her to stick around after hours.

It's almost time. The words repeated themselves over and over in Allison's head.

As the main factory floor completely emptied of the remaining workers, who had been cleaning up their stations, Allison stepped back into a dark corner with her broom. It appeared that no one was left in the room except the guard standing on the deck of the nuclear reactor. She waited for what seemed like forever.

All was officially clear when, based on the time, all workers should have cleared the building. The lights in the halls automatically shut themselves off one by one. All that remained for light now was a dim ray shining over the guard. Allison crept out of her corner, broom in hand, and slowly made her way to the back of the nuclear reactor deck. *It's time.* The words rang in Allison's head before going silent.

The stairs of the deck stood before her as Allison clenched the broom handle tightly. She took a deep breath, her eyes flashing from worry to anger in a moment. She ascended the stairs carefully so as not to alert the guard to her presence.

The guard suddenly walked over to the opening at the top of the stairs. Allison ducked out of sight against the reactor staircase railing just in time. The guard stood motionless, looked around him, then began to descend the staircase. He appeared not to notice her leaning against the railing.

Allison knew this was her moment. As the guard began to walk past her, she raised her arm to knock him over the head. But he spun around and blocked her arm with his. He punched her in the jaw.

The guard pinned Allison's arms above her head as he fumbled for his taser. She managed to free one of her arms from his powerful grasp and belted him in the head with her hand, the metal fingers and palm crashing together as the guard gave a muffled yelp. His body went limp and he fell down the remaining stairs, coming to rest motionless on the cement floor below.

Allison stood there looking at the figure below and rubbed her jaw. "Almost done," she said to herself, before climbing the remaining stairs and entering the deck.

She rushed across to the control panel and looked for the danger-level lever. Once she spotted it, she lifted it until the needle went from low to high. The reactor began to squeal at a higher and higher pitch as the needle went past the high level and onto the final danger level.

Allison backed away from the control panel, angrily staring at it as sirens began to shriek all over the room. As she turned to leave, she found herself face-to-face with John M.

"You crazy bitch!" he hissed at her, swinging a punch at her face. She dodged his blow and threw the broom, which she was surprised to find was still in her hand, at him with great force. He caught it, snapped the handle over his knee, and held out one of the broken ends, which had formed a sharp spear.

Allison stood between John M. and the reactor control panel. He lunged toward her to get to the panel. She stopped him by grabbing the broomstick spear and pulverizing it with one clench of her hand.

He grabbed her by the throat and managed to knock her to the ground. He got on top of her, beads of sweat dripping from his forehead as the heat of the reactor increased. "You'll pay for this with your life, miss!" he exclaimed maniacally.

Allison winced up into his sweaty face as she gasped for air. "Yes . . ." she started to say. John M. looked at her quizzically. "Sir!" she finished.

John M.'s eyes widened as she grabbed his chest and pushed him over the railing around the deck. He plummeted onto the cement below with a howl of pain and lay panting on the ground.

Allison stood up and looked down at him. "Now you know what it feels like to be the one on the ground, sir!" she screamed at him as she ran from the deck and descended the staircase.

The reactor hissed so loudly now that they could hear nothing else. John M. stood up shakily and looked at it.

"It's too late now!" he yelled to himself and began to limp away as fast as he could after Allison.

Allison rushed out into the main hallway toward the front entrance of Omega. As she began to exit through the door, John M. slammed her into the glass from behind.

The glass door shattered, sending them out into the snowbank outside. The same snowbank Allison had found Mia lying in. She grabbed John M.'s face and buried his head in the snowbank. "This is for Mia, you sick toerag!" she cried, her voice shaking as tears and blood streamed down her face.

John M. managed to get his head free and looked up into Allison's face as she stood towering over him. "You'll never get out of Omega alive, girly," he whispered, an evil smirk on his lips.

Allison paused for a moment, breathing heavily. She turned and began to run toward her car in the parking lot.

"You'll never get out of Omega alive!" screamed John M. again.

As Allison reached her car and hopped into the driver's seat, she fumbled for the keys in her pocket. "These freaking hands!" she exclaimed, barely managing to grasp the key and put it into the ignition.

The car started, and Allison pushed the pedal to the floor. The Beetle spun its tires on the icy pavement but managed to start picking up forward momentum. Allison looked behind her to see whether John M. was still there; he was nowhere to be seen.

Once she was as far away from the building as she thought was safe, she pulled the car to the side of the road. She got out and looked back at the small black spot that was the Omega building. "It should have gone off by now," she said to herself.

Suddenly, a flash of bright white light bleached the sky and the view all around. Allison screamed as she felt her eyes burning. She stumbled back into the car and slammed the door behind her. The vehicle began to tremble violently as it lifted into the air and rolled over into a roadside ditch. The blast that came from Omega swept across the miles and miles of open land around it with a strong, hot gust of wind.

Lying in the mangled Beetle, Allison cried out in pain when she rubbed her eyes. Then the world went dark as she fainted, alone in the vast fields that surrounded Omega . . . which was no more.

Christmas decorations lined the streets and shopfronts of Allison's hometown. Pedestrians were absent during this time of the night as the moon rose into the sky and light sprinkles of snowflakes fell to the ground. From out of the snowy view just outside the streetlights came the figure of Allison trudging through the cold. By this time, the cold had settled into her body, and her eyes felt dry and bloodshot. She could see, but she felt a searing pain every time she blinked.

"Idiot!" she muttered to herself. "You shouldn't have looked back! You know this!"

Allison saw up ahead, as she walked down the empty street, the lights of the corner grocery store were on. The store was the only place in town open this late. She decided to get something to eat on the way home.

When she entered the store, she spotted a man in tattered clothes yelling in a drunken stupor at the clerk behind the counter. She decided to ignore the situation and move on to the frozen dinner aisle. Allison grabbed a couple of meals carefully so as not to crush the packaging with her hands and made her way back to the checkout counter. The drunk man was still present, yelling at the top of his voice at the clerk, who stood helpless behind the counter.

Allison stood behind the drunk man, somewhat annoyed since all she wanted to do was pay for her food and leave as quickly as possible. He turned around and looked up into Allison's bloodshot eyes, which now had a hint of a yellow in her retinas. "You got a problem?" he slurred.

"No," replied Allison tiredly. "It's been a long day, and I was in a car accident. I don't mean to butt in on your issue, but I would like to pay for my goods and leave, if you please."

The drunk man slobbered and brushed her off as he turned back to the clerk. In a sudden fit of rage, he grabbed a soup can from the counter and hurled it at the clerk. The clerk tried to duck but fell to the floor as it bounced off his head.

"Get out!" the clerk shouted, rubbing his forehead.

The drunken man tried to start another spat but was stopped by a cold hand from Allison firmly on his shoulder. He turned around and looked into Allison's icy stare. He backed away slowly and stumbled out the door.

Allison helped the clerk off the floor and asked him if he was okay. He said he was, so she paid for her items before walking out into the wintry night.

As Allison walked down the street toward her home, she shuddered from the cold. The ache of hunger was rising in her stomach. "What a day," she mumbled to herself.

She rounded a bend in the street and came upon an alleyway. She always disliked this shortcut to her home, but she decided to take it anyway. It was very dark, but the white light of the moon managed to dimly illuminate what lay ahead. She could see a pile of garbage to her left.

Suddenly the drunk man from the store leapt out of the garbage pile, blocking her way. "Trying to muscle me back there, missy?" he growled at Allison.

Allison, after a quick jolt at his surprise appearance, rolled her eyes and sighed. "Sir, I just want to get home. If you'll just let me pass, I'll be on my way."

"No one makes a fool out of me except me!" exclaimed the man. He began to push her backward in defiance.

Allison at first thought this was comical—after all, the man stood about a foot and a half shorter than her, so he basically had to push her by the stomach as he stumbled in a drunken stupor. "Go home and sleep it off," she said.

The man swung at her face. Allison had had enough. She set her groceries down and put her hand on the man's face and pushed him back into the garbage off to the side. The man, enraged now, grabbed a switchblade from his tattered overcoat and pointed it in her direction.

"Everyone is so violent these days," said Allison.

The man lunged at her, knife above his head, ready to strike. When the two met, Allison reached for his face and gripped his forehead tightly. The man groaned as the cold metal fingers of her hand began to tighten.

Allison felt a sudden surge of adrenaline overcome her, and she squeezed tighter. The man's forehead collapsed under her grip. Blood and brain matter oozed all over her hand as she lowered it, leaving four large gashes down what remained of the man's head.

The figure fell to the ground limply. After a minute or so of looking at the body at her feet, Allison wiped her hand off in the snow and picked up her groceries. She quickly walked off down the alley and onto the street on which she lived. After retrieving her keys, she unlocked the door and stepped inside her home. She quickly shut the door behind her and locked it, and then leaned against it and closed her eyes as tears began to stream down her face.

Allison warmed up one of the microwave meals and sat down at the table. She cracked open a bottle of ginger ale by twisting the cap off with her finger as if it was a bottle opener. As the cold liquid reached her throat, she heard whimpering and something scratching at her front door. Puzzled, she stood up to investigate. She walked into the living room, past the boxed-up Christmas tree and decorations that waited to be unpacked, and slowly opened the door.

There, on the snow-covered front stoop, sat a puppy. It had scraggly hair, and its tongue hung loosely from the side of its mouth. It was shivering and whimpering as it looked up at the now pajama-clad Allison.

"Oh, you poor thing!" she exclaimed. She knelt and picked it up into her arms. "Come inside and warm up."

Allison shut the door behind her and brought the puppy into the kitchen. After retrieving a bowl from the cupboard, she filled it with water. The still-shivering puppy started lapping up the water as she set down the bowl on the floor by it.

"You were thirsty!" she said. "Are you hungry?"

The puppy looked up and wagged its tail excitedly.

"Let's see what I've got in the pantry," she said as she opened the pantry door. "I don't have any dog food, but I have to have something in here you'll probably eat."

She pulled out a can of chunky beef stew and poured it into another bowl. Before she could even set it down on the floor, the puppy was already frantically at the food.

"Poor little thing," whispered Allison. "Do you have a home? Why were you out in the cold this late at night?" The puppy looked up at her and whimpered. "Well, I guess you can stay here tonight until someone comes to ask about you," said Allison, petting the puppy's head.

Allison sat down to finish her meal as the puppy finished his. She cleaned up the dishes and walked into the living room with the puppy at her heels.

"Want to help me set up the Christmas tree?" she asked. The two went about getting the tree and ornaments set up in the room, and Allison put on a Phil Spector Christmas vinyl to help with the ambiance.

As she hung the ornaments on the tree, Allison looked at some of them and thought about the times as a little girl hanging them with her parents. She missed them dearly. The puppy looked up, watched her as she sighed, and rubbed his face against her leg.

Allison picked the puppy up and sat down on the couch in the dark room. The only light in the house now was what emanated from the tree. Allison and the puppy lay down on the couch and fell asleep in the warmth of the home as a blizzard began to whirl outside.

The morning sun glistened on the icicles that lined the roof of Allison's home. She slowly opened her eyes and looked at the puppy snoozing in her arms on the couch. She noticed that her eyes felt much better than they had the night before, so she was glad for that. After slowly rising to her feet so as not to wake the puppy snoring as it lay, she walked to the bathroom to clean up for the day.

When she looked in the mirror, she stood back aghast. The retinas of her eyes were a glowing, phosphorescent yellow! "I can see just fine," she said to herself. "It must have been from the light of the blast yesterday. I've never heard of radiation exposure aftereffect symptoms such as this, but mutations are known to happen. Maybe it will go away soon." She showered and dressed.

When she entered the living room, she looked at her piano in the corner. She walked over to it and stood motionless in thought. She pulled out the bench, sat down at the piano, and raised her hands to play a chord. The result was a discordant crash. Allison pushed the hair from her face and sighed in frustration. Her lips trembled. "All the years of practice . . . gone forever," she murmured to herself.

The puppy awoke, scampered off the couch to Allison's side, and whimpered. Allison sniffed and smiled at the little one whining up at her. She took it outside to go to the bathroom.

Once breakfast was eaten and cleaned up, Allison turned on the television. The news was on.

"Important updates concerning the disaster at the site of the now former Omega Corporation . . . It is with sadness that we announce its closure without plans for any near future rebuild in our community due to the radioactive fallout levels now associated with the area. Omega Corporation officials do say, however, that they plan to rebuild in another state in about two years' time.

"From the explosion yesterday, only three fatalities were reported this morning: foreman John Mortimer of Sheppertown County, security guard Kyle Gently, and production worker Allison Finkle . . ."

Allison glanced up at the TV.

The reporter continued, "It is believed that Allison Finkle tried to escape the building, since her vehicle was found destroyed just outside of the blast impact, but her body was obliterated by the aftershock and fallout. Foreman John Mortimer was reported missing by his friends after work yesterday, and we are certain Kyle Gently was killed and his remains were destroyed in the explosion, since his post was at the nuclear reactor.

"If we learn anything more, we will update you. In the meantime, just go about your daily business and stay clear of the fields near the site where the Omega Corporation once stood. That is all."

Allison turned from the TV and sat down on the couch.

"I'm dead," she said to the puppy sitting next to her. "I need to come up with a new identity if I'm going to continue to survive in this world and continue my experiments."

The puppy looked up at her quizzically.

"What kind of a name should I go by? What should be my identity in relation to Allison Finkle?" Allison asked herself and the puppy. "Because if anyone recognizes me, I should probably say I'm Allison's long-lost twin or something."

The puppy barked and licked her metal hand.

"That's gross," said Allison, chuckling.

She looked up and noticed a copy of book four of *Metamorphoses* by the Roman poet Ovid on the coffee table near the couch. She picked up the book and started skimming through the pages. She came upon the story of Perseus and Andromeda and Perseus's defeat of the mighty sea monster using the head of Medusa, the gorgon, turning the beast into stone and saving Andromeda.

"Andromeda . . ." said Allison to herself.

The TV across the room continued the news coverage on the status of the fallout created by the bomb blast at the Omega Corporation. Allison's eyes widened, the bright yellow retinas began to sparkle with a kind of glee, and then a glint of mischief crossed them. She looked down at the puppy.

"Fallout," she said to the animal. "Andromeda . . . Fallout."

The puppy stood up and wagged its tail.

"Dr. Andromeda Fallout!" exclaimed Allison to the puppy, hugging it to her chest.

"I have my PhD! From here on out I'll be Dr. Andromeda Fallout!"

Andromeda stood up and looked down at the puppy. "Come with me!" she said and picked up the little dog.

Entering the kitchen, Andromeda pulled a switch under the kitchen island. The island mechanically moved over the floor, exposing a secret staircase beneath. They descended the steps, which led down into a large, dark room. Andromeda turned on a light switch at the base of the stairs. A bright ceiling lamp illuminated the room, exposing a laboratory with lots of test tubes and machines.

"This is my she-shed, dog," said Andromeda to the animal in her arms.

She set the puppy down and walked over to a cabinet. "I think I might have a collar or something in here for you, dog," said Andromeda. The puppy barked excitedly and waddled over to her feet and sat down.

"I remember years ago when I was young," continued Andromeda, "that I attempted to make a collar for animals that would help them to be able to speak. But my parents wouldn't let me get a dog and none of my friends had one, so I couldn't test it out."

The puppy sat panting in anticipation as Andromeda pulled an old black collar from the top shelf. She blew the dust off it and knelt by the animal. The puppy sat patiently as she fastened the collar around its neck. She pushed a button on a small black box on the collar, which beeped.

"It's supposed to take any vocal vibrations you make and sense any emotions based on your physical reactions," she said to the puppy. "I don't know. It might not work. I never tried it—"

"Seems to be working quite well!" interrupted a voice from the puppy.

"Whoa!" exclaimed Andromeda, falling back onto her bottom in surprise.

"I can speak, so you can understand me!" shouted the puppy happily. "This is so cool! Totally cool!"

"I'm amazed I didn't have to do any calibrations or tests on it. I figured I would have had to," said Andromeda.

The puppy jumped onto her lap. "I don't have an owner by the way," said the puppy. "I escaped the pound truck when I was separated from my family in an alley in another town."

"Well, you are more than welcome to stay with me," whispered Andromeda, hugging the animal.

"What's my name?" asked the puppy.

"I don't know yet," replied Andromeda.

"You got to choose a cool new name," said the puppy. "I want a cool name too. Something technical and smart sounding. After all, you're a doctor and have this lab and stuff."

"Something technical, huh?" thought Andromeda, rubbing her chin.

The two sat on the floor in silence for a few moments.

"I've got it!" exclaimed the puppy suddenly.

"What?" asked Andromeda wide-eyed.

"My name is one I've chosen for myself," said the puppy.

"I'm well aware of that," laughed Andromeda.

"My name is . . ." started the puppy.

Andromeda rolled her eyes impatiently.

"TURD!" yelled the puppy, holding his paw proudly to his chest.

Andromeda sat back against the desk behind her and put her hand to her forehead while belly laughing.

"What's so funny?" murmured the puppy.

"How in the world did you come up with a name like *that*?" asked Andromeda, trying to regain her composure.

"I am your Technically Universal Reserve Dog," replied the animal. "So TURD is my name, and TURD it shall be, you see."

Andromeda petted the puppy's head and tried not to chuckle. "Okay, Turd," she agreed as she stood back up. "Turd it is, then."

Turd barked, stood up, and wagged his tail happily. "As your sidekick now, Dr. Andromeda Fallout, what is the next step in our adventure?" asked Turd.

"I think we should enjoy the remainder of this Christmas season," replied Andromeda. "And the first thing we should do is to go out for a walk and get a tag made for your collar."

"Woo-hoo!" exclaimed Turd excitedly as he and Andromeda scaled the steps.

Andromeda moved the island counter back over the exposed secret stairwell and grabbed her coat and mittens.

"What is the point of you wearing mittens?" asked Turd, perplexed. "You can't feel the cold with your hands anyway. Can you?"

"I've got to hide my hands in public, at least for now," replied Andromeda.

"Why?" asked Turd.

"In case I get noticed by any authorities who might think to question me about working for Omega because of them," replied Andromeda. "The plant was destroyed yesterday, as you saw on the TV, and I need to stay on the down-low for now."

"You blew the joint up, didn't you?" asked Turd, a sly smirk crossing his lips.

"Yes, I did," replied Andromeda seriously as she put a pair of pitch-black sunglasses over her yellow eyes. "And you better swear to me that you'll never tell."

"Mum's the word, master," answered the dog.

"Call me Andromeda or Doc, please," mumbled Andromeda as she stood by the front door. "Master is way too diabolical sounding. Like what the bad guy's sidekick or Renfield from Dracula would say."

"Okey dokey, Doc," said Turd as the two walked out the front door into the early afternoon light.

The town appeared empty and peaceful this afternoon, which was interesting to Andromeda, since the mayhem from the previous day was all over the news. She expected people to be in a tizzy, but apparently they weren't. Taking advantage of the peace and quiet, the two walked down the sidewalk, enjoying the Christmas ambiance of decorations lining the streets on the lampposts.

"So, where are we going to get the tag for my collar?" asked Turd.

"There's a place just at the end of the center of town called Mark's Bar and General Store," replied Andromeda. "Mark should be able to hook us up with a dog tag."

The two arrived at the bar and store as snow began to sprinkle down on them. Andromeda opened the door, setting off the entrance bell, and stepped inside with Turd. They stamped their snow-covered feet off on the doormat as a young woman with long icy-blond hair, wearing a striped shirt and baggy Tripp pants, greeted them.

"Oh, hi!" said the woman cheerfully. "How can I help you today?"

"Where's Mark?" asked Andromeda confused. She had never seen this woman before. "Who are you?"

"Oh, I'm so sorry," apologized the woman. "My name is Audrey. I'm Mark's new assistant here at the store and bar."

"Nice to meet you," said Andromeda. "My dog here needs a tag for his collar."

"Any special kind? We have a lot of different tag options here now," said Audrey as she motioned Andromeda and Turd over to the pet area.

"My dog loves Elvis," said Andromeda. "Especially the '68 Comeback Concert. So, I was hoping for some bedazzling with the tag."

"Who's Elvis?" asked Turd.

"You love Elvis, Turd," replied Andromeda. "Remember? Especially when you're upset and need me to hold you while I play Elvis records."

Turd looked at her in puzzlement but figured it was part of their new cover story, so he went along with it.

"Very cool that your dog can talk!" exclaimed Audrey as a man approached the group from another aisle.

The man had long, black rocker-style hair and a strange accent. It was Mark.

"Hello," said Andromeda.

"Oh, hi, Allison," replied Mark. "What you come in for today?"

"My name is not Allison," said Andromeda quickly—she had almost forgotten her new identity.

"Yeah, you Allison," retorted Mark in his broken English, very confused.

"No, actually, I'm Allison's twin sister," explained Andromeda as nonchalantly as possible. "I came to town when I heard about my sister Allison's death in the Omega Corporation disaster yesterday.

Our parents are both dead, so I'm currently staying at the family home with my dog."

"Oh, wow, really?" asked Mark. "Seem like you and her look very much alike. I so sorry for the confusion and your loss."

"They came in today to get a tag for a dog collar," said Audrey to Mark. "What was the dog's name again?"

"My name is Turd," said Turd bluntly.

"Why you named Turd?" laughed Mark. Audrey clutched Mark's arm and winced at his rude laughter at the customers.

"It's complicated," retorted Turd.

"You could at least pretend you love my dog's name," mumbled Andromeda to Mark.

"I so sorry for laughing," said Mark. "I have just the tag for you guys at no charge."

"Thank you, Mark," responded Andromeda, letting a smile cross her lips.

After having the new dog tag made for Turd, Andromeda and the puppy left the store after thanking Mark and Audrey for their help. Turd rather liked his shiny new tag, which glistened in the wintery sunlight. They walked down the sidewalk in the middle of town, looking in the shop windows as they went.

"We should probably have gotten you some actual dog food, Turd, when we were at Mark's," said Andromeda to the animal at her side.

"Glad you didn't," mumbled Turd. "I rather liked that people food last night."

Andromeda and Turd stopped at a crosswalk and waited for the light to change. A man bundled up against the cold approached them and stood waiting as well. Andromeda glanced through her dark sunglasses at the figure's face. For some reason, she felt she recognized the man, but his face was covered with a scarf. She looked away and brushed aside the thought.

When the light changed, she began to cross the road when the light changed. As the three reached the other side of the road, the man slipped and fell onto his back with a loud grunt. Turd yelped in surprise and Andromeda quickly bent over to help. She carefully grabbed the man's hand with her mitten-covered ones and helped him to his feet.

"Are you all right, sir?" asked Andromeda.

The man growled and grunted as he pulled the scarf from his face. It was John M.!

"Ugh! I lost my job yesterday to an idiot. I'm homeless at the moment because of it! Only to wind up with a broken back the day after!" he said, red faced.

Andromeda gulped as she felt her insides fall in shock. She managed to maintain her composure. Turd looked up at her carefully from the corner of his eye and remained silent.

"I . . . I am so sorry, sir!" she stammered, choking on her words. "Are you sure your back is okay?"

"I think so," replied John M. with a huff. "No harm done. It was my fault anyway. Bad luck, I guess."

Andromeda thought quickly. This was her chance to see if John M. would recognize her.

"May I ask you what happened yesterday with your job, sir?" she asked. "Yesterday I lost my sister, Allison, in the Omega Corporation explosion. Is that where you worked? You remind me of the man I saw on the news. They said a man disappeared during the disaster and they assumed he was dead."

"Yes, that was me," answered John M. "I was in management there. You'll have to forgive my abruptness, but it was your sister who destroyed Omega and tried to kill me!"

"What?" exclaimed Andromeda, doing her best to sound shocked.

"Yes! Your sister was crazy! And if she had survived, she would more than likely have received the death penalty for her actions!" snarled John M.

"I had no idea," murmured Andromeda.

"You look just like her, miss," said John M. "If I didn't know better, I would have thought you *were* Allison. What is your name?"

"I'm Allison's identical twin sister, Andromeda," stuttered Andromeda. "Many have said we look very much alike. No one could tell us apart growing up."

Turd nervously rolled his eyes at the lies but remained alert to the story she was telling.

"Are you from out of town?" asked John M. "I'm surprised you didn't end up working at Omega as well."

"I'm from another state," replied Andromeda. "I just came back with my dog when I saw the news."

"Interesting," smirked John M. "Well, even though your sister was crazy, we got along quite well up until the end."

Andromeda felt an angry lump develop in her throat. It made her feel like vomiting all over the man's face. She swallowed hard and said, "That is too bad. I'm mortified to know she went crazy there."

"And to think of all I did for her and could have given her," continued John M., sighing dramatically.

"I'm sure," remarked Andromeda sharply. "But anyway, my sister is dead, and I need to get home and get my dog out of the cold. It was nice to meet you, sir."

"My pleasure to meet you as well," said John M. with a perverted glint in his eye. "Maybe I can take you to dinner sometime?"

Andromeda stopped cold at the question. She wanted to be out of this man's presence more than anything as she felt a great rage boil up inside her. She wanted to kill him right then and there as flashbacks of Omega, Mia, and her treatment flooded her brain. After a short pause, she forced a smile onto her face. "Why, that would be very nice," she said politely. "Maybe I can ask you a few questions about my sister then too. And learn more about you?"

Turd watched this sudden change of heart in Andromeda with confusion.

"Of course!" said John M., now a bit more smoothly. "I would be glad to. And to get to know the beautiful sister of a beautiful woman like your sister was."

Andromeda tried to force her herself to look flirtatious. "Thank you for the compliment, sir," she said.

"Please, call me John M.," said John M.

"Okay, John M.," said Andromeda in almost a whisper. "Would you like to meet for dinner tonight?"

"I sure would, baby," said John M.

Andromeda wanted to laugh at this man's sickening forwardness. "Well, can we get dinner this evening at Mark's Bar? Six o'clock?" she whispered.

"Sounds good to me . . . baby," grunted John M.

"I'll see you then, John M.," said Andromeda. She bit her lip as playfully as she could.

John M.'s eyes widened with lust as Andromeda turned away from him and walked away with Turd by her side. As she rounded the corner, she looked back once at the man standing on the sidewalk before she was out of his sight. Once they had walked about ten feet, Andromeda and Turd sprinted down the road to their house. They didn't stop until the door was shut and locked behind them.

"What in the world was *that*?" asked Turd, perplexed.

"I don't know exactly!" replied Andromeda, panting. "All I know is I have him wrapped around my little metal finger!"

"*Why* would you want *that*?" continued Turd.

"He killed my friend Mia. He was a horrendous human being to me at Omega! He's the one who cut my hands off!" explained Andromeda, shaking.

"Oh," murmured Turd.

Andromeda leaned against the door and stared blankly at the room in thought.

"So," asked Turd, "what are you going to do?"

"I'm going to kill him," answered Andromeda with a fire in her eyes. "I'm going to kill him—tonight. It's over for that bastard."

"What do you want me to do?" continued Turd. "Do you have a plan I need to be a part of? I'd do anything for you, Doc."

"I know you would, Turd," said Andromeda calmly as she gently patted the animal's head. "If I end up bringing him back home with me tonight after dinner, play along with whatever I tell you to do. As my pet. Okay?"

"You got it," answered Turd.

The moon rose over the thin winter clouds that floated across the night sky. Andromeda stood in front of the bathroom mirror while she applied her makeup. She had wondered all afternoon how she was going to hide her prostheses from John M. She knew he would know she was Allison if he saw those hands of hers.

After much deliberation and many failures trying on dress gloves in her wardrobe, she decided to keep her hands in her pockets and hope for the best. It was all she could do. Her hands were simply too clunky to hide without bulky mittens or pockets. Her eyes were no longer the color they were before the explosion. The bright, glowing yellow in her retinas, she figured, was different enough for her to make up some story about them if John M. asked her.

All Andromeda had at this moment in time was the angry drive to rid her life of this man. If that meant having to do it in Mark's bar, right there in front of onlookers, she would, but she hoped that wouldn't be the case. She sighed and teased her hair a little before exiting the bathroom and entering her bedroom, where she dressed for the date.

Turd was sitting on the couch watching an old 1940s Christmas movie when Andromeda entered the room and sat down next to him.

"You look nice—for a human that is, Doc," Turd complimented Andromeda as she slipped on her knee-high dress boots.

"Thanks," said Andromeda. "I haven't had a date in so many years. Too bad it's not even a romantic one."

"I don't understand. Why wouldn't you have lots of dates all the time?" asked Turd.

"I was in school. Very focused on my studies," answered Andromeda. "And my first real date after being home, of course, has to be a deadly mission."

"Okay, cool," said Turd. He picked at his nose with his paw.

"Gross," mumbled Andromeda as she stood up to put her coat on.

"I'll be ready whenever you get back to the house," said Turd.

Andromeda smiled at the dog and walked to the front door. "See you later, Turd," she said with a sigh.

"Sounds good," answered Turd with his eyes glued to the TV.

The night chill met Andromeda's face as she opened the door and stepped outside. It was almost six o'clock, so she walked briskly into town to Mark's Bar.

When Andromeda arrived in town, she watched a young couple enjoying themselves as they whizzed past her down the street in a horse-drawn sleigh. "Merry Christmas," she said quietly to herself, since the couple wouldn't be able to hear her.

Mark's Bar and General Store was lit up beautifully with lights all over the fascia of the building. Andromeda breathed in deeply as she opened the door and stepped inside. The bar was empty, save Mark and Audrey sitting behind the counter.

"Hello, Mark and Audrey," Andromeda said.

"Welcome to my bar!" exclaimed Mark. "Audrey? Will you show our guest to one of the tables, please?"

Audrey greeted Andromeda sweetly and showed her to one of the empty tables. "Will there be two of you?" asked Audrey.

"Yes," replied Andromeda. "My date should be here any minute, I would think. We agreed to meet at six o'clock."

"Would you like something to drink while you wait?" asked Audrey.

"No, thank you. I'll just wait." Andromeda smiled.

Audrey nodded, walked back over to the bar, and started to chat with Mark.

Minutes passed, then an hour. Andromeda began to get anxious. She remained careful, however, not to expose her hands by taking them out of her pockets.

Audrey walked up to her table. "Looks like your date ditched you?" she asked Andromeda.

"Looks to be that way," replied Andromeda.

At that second, a man burst through the bar door and stumbled in from the cold. It was John M., and he appeared to be drunk. "I'm . . . here!" he stammered.

Andromeda and Audrey looked up in surprise at his sudden appearance. Audrey pursed her lips and looked over at Mark. Andromeda looked at John M., trying not to show her fury. Behind the bar, Mark put his hand to his forehead and sighed.

"Hey, baby!" slurred John M. "I wanted to be fashionably late! Nothing more attractive than being fashionably late to keep the lady in suspense!"

Andromeda glared at John M. and gritted her teeth as he stiffly walked over to the table and sat down.

Audrey came over with some drinks. After both declined a meal, she left the two to talk.

"I'm glad you were still able to make it," said Andromeda as sweetly as she could.

"Yes, it's cold, and I got stuck at a joint on the other end of town," said John M.

Andromeda gazed into John M.'s eyes and leaned forward in her chair. She knew she had him in her pocket, given his condition and the emptiness of the bar. But she didn't really want to do it in front of Mark and Audrey. She liked them, and it wasn't their fault that she had a history with the monster sitting across from her. They didn't need to see or have a murder in their quaint little place.

"All of this waiting has made me . . . you know . . . just want to be alone with you," said Andromeda seductively.

John M. leaned back in his chair. "Oh yeah . . . baby?" he said in a whisper.

"Yes," whispered Andromeda, biting her bottom lip while still gazing intently into the man's eyes.

"Let's go to your place then . . . baby," said John M.

Andromeda held in her annoyance at being called "baby" this much and slowly stood up. John M. stood and looked up at the towering woman beside him.

"You may be a foot taller than me, like your sister," said John M, "but give me five minutes and I'll change your life forever."

Andromeda forced a blush to her face and smiled as if she was embarrassed. "Well, let's get out of here," she said with a wink.

Andromeda held out the crook of her arm—her hands were still in her pockets—and

John M. linked his arm with hers as they left the bar.

Mark and Audrey stood silent as they watched the door shut behind Andromeda and John M. "She gonna kill him," said Mark abruptly.

"What?" asked Audrey wide-eyed.

"Yeah," continued Mark, "she gonna kill him. That John M. from Omega, and that Allison who worked there. She now is Andromeda and gonna take revenge tonight."

"How do you know all this?" asked Audrey as she raised an eyebrow.

"I'm not a little bit stupid guy," replied Mark, glancing into Audrey's questioning eyes. "I know more than I let others know."

Audrey put her arms around Mark's shoulders. "Is that why I'm attracted to you?" she asked playfully, before planting a kiss on Mark's lips.

"Yeah," replied Mark, "when you are a thousand-and-one-year-old vampire, you know things others don't."

They winked at each other and embraced.

Andromeda and John M. walked down the street toward her home. Adrenaline raced through her veins as John M. hung onto the crook of her arm while they trekked through the snowy streets. When they reached Andromeda's front stoop, she opened the door carefully.

"I'm home, Turd!" she called out to her dog.

Turd ran up to the door, barking, as the couple entered the room. Andromeda looked Turd in the eyes, and the dog grimaced back. He walked over to John M.'s leg and rubbed his back on it.

"Get away, dog!" yelled John M., pushing the puppy away from him.

Turd yelped, rushed across the room, and jumped on the couch.

"Now, Turd," said Andromeda in a playfully condescending tone, "this is our guest. His name is John M., and he doesn't like to be given such attention."

Turd barked, lay down on the couch, and whimpered. Andromeda winked at him as she and John M. strode past the couch. Turd winked back at her.

As they entered Andromeda's bedroom, John M. sat on the bed and rubbed his face. Andromeda looked down at him with a crazed look in her eyes. "Let me slip into something more comfortable, if you don't mind," she said and walked to the bathroom. John M. snorted and started to take his jacket off.

In the bathroom, Andromeda stripped down to her bra and underwear and looked at herself in the mirror. "I can't believe this is how far things had to go," she whispered to herself. "This is disgusting. But it'll be over soon . . . I hope." She teased her hair with her hands and shook it back and forth.

After giving herself a smooch in the mirror, Andromeda went back toward the bedroom. She clasped her hands behind her back as she slowly strode toward the bedroom door. She carefully pushed the door open with her shoulder.

The room was lit by single candle, and John M. was lying on the bed with his head propped up on his arm.

"I'm back," said Andromeda quietly.

"Come to me, baby," whispered John M.

Andromeda casually walked up to the bed, trying to look cute. John M. kneeled on the mattress and looked into her eyes. He placed his hand gently on her cheek, and their lips touched. Andromeda hesitated at first but sighed and went in for the kiss.

"What beautiful eyes you have," whispered John M. "I've never seen eyes like yours before. They are like glowing beacons of phosphorus."

"Thank . . . you," Andromeda stammered.

John M. pulled her onto the bed next to him—she was careful to keep her hands hidden in the blankets—and kissed her passionately. He stroked his hand along the side of her bare torso and she tensed as if enjoying it.

"Take your shirt off," ordered Andromeda, breathing heavily.

"No," answered John M. "I have a large mole on my chest, and I like to keep it covered."

Andromeda's eyes widened as she managed to hold in a belly laugh. "Are you worried I might get it snagged in my teeth or something?" she giggled.

"Maybe," whispered John M. as he continued to basically eat her face and neck.

"I . . . I . . . need to catch my breath," gasped Andromeda, and sat up.

"We've barely even started," said John M., annoyed.

By the flickering candlelight, Andromeda turned her head toward John M. Her eyes were sparkling with almost crazed anticipation. "Yes, we've barely even started," she said seriously. "You'll never get out of here alive."

John M. looked back at her questioningly.

"Interesting, isn't it," Andromeda continued, "how something like the Omega disaster brought us back together? According to your own words, I was never going to get out of Omega alive. Now you, sir, will never get out of *here* alive."

"What are you talking about?" asked John M.

Andromeda's face worked itself into a sly grin as she continued to lock eyes with John M.

"ALLISON FINKLE! IT'S YOU!" cried John M., shock and anger raging inside him.

"*Doctor Andromeda Fallout to you!*" hissed Andromeda, fire raging in her eyes.

She jerked her arm out from under the blanket and slammed her metal hand into John M.'s face. He grabbed her arm, stunned, yanked it away, and kicked her off the bed. Andromeda fell to the floor, hitting her head against the dresser. John M., groaning angrily, got up onto the bed.

"I'm blind! I can't see out of my eye!" he howled.

Andromeda, in the dim light, saw one of his eyes hanging out of its socket. She rubbed her head where it hit the dresser and leapt up.

"Does that hurt you?" Andromeda growled. "Like it hurt me when you hacked my hands off?"

John M. slid off the bed and staggered to his feet, swinging a punch at her.

"Or when you killed my friend Mia?" continued Andromeda. "When you left her to freeze to death in the cold?"

"It was work policy!" hissed John M. He managed to grab her by the throat and pin her against the wall. "She was a useless employee anyway!"

"Then I will give *you* corrections, my dear sir!" snarled Andromeda, gritting her teeth. She grabbed John M.'s head between her hands as he continued to tighten his grip on her throat.

"You're fired . . . sir," she said as her hands came together with a loud metallic clap.

John M.'s headless body fell to the floor like a sack of potatoes. Andromeda stood over him with blood and the contents of his head dripping from her hands onto the floor. She fell to her knees and convulsively wept as she scooted away from the body.

Turd poked his head into the doorway of the room. "Is the coast clear?" he asked in a whisper.

Andromeda, leaning against the wall, sat on the floor shaking, with tears streaming down her face. "It's over," she whimpered. "It's finally over."

The puppy walked into the room and lay down next to her as silence filled the air . . . and the candle burned itself out.

It was Christmas Eve and a couple of days after the death of John M. Andromeda and Turd had disposed of his body in the incinerator in her basement laboratory.

Andromeda and Turd fiddled around silently in the lab as they worked on Andromeda's experiments on the neutralization of bomb explosion damage and the effects of fallout. She had begun to make improvements to a theory on forms of implosion as an antidote to explosions. Of course, all of this was only on paper, but Andromeda had begun to plan a means of containing her antidote formula in tiny capsules that could be planted near nuclear and atomic testing sites and factories as a means of emergency backup in case of an accident. She couldn't wait to field test these new devices after New Year, when the weather permitted.

"Well, Turd," said Andromeda to the puppy, "that should do it for now with the experiments. Let's take a breather. After all, it's Christmas Eve. Let's try to enjoy it."

"Sounds good to me!" barked Turd.

Just then, the doorbell rang upstairs. Andromeda and Turd quickly exited the basement and closed the secret stairwell.

Andromeda walked to the front door and opened it. There, standing on the front stoop, were Mark and Audrey. They were bundled up in long, fluffy black coats and holding a tray of cookies.

"Merry Christmas," said Audrey in a small, shivering voice.

"Oh, wow. You cold or something?" asked Mark as he turned toward Audrey.

"I'm always cold . . . or something," replied Audrey, rolling her eyes.

Andromeda quickly invited them into the house and out of the cold.

"We just thought we would stop by to bring some cookies to you and Turd before tomorrow," said Audrey pleasantly.

"Thank you so much!" smiled Andromeda. "We really appreciate the gesture."

"You guys are welcome to Mark's Bar tomorrow for Christmas dinner," said Mark in his broken English.

"Should we bring anything?" asked Turd.

"Just yourselves," replied Audrey, patting the dog on the head.

"That would be lovely," said Andromeda.

After the two visitors warmed up a little and drank hot chocolate, they decided to head back into town.

"That guy with you the other day," asked Mark when he was halfway out the door. "He gone now, right?"

"Oh! Ugh . . ." stammered Andromeda, trying to find the words. "Y-yes, he is gone now. A one-date deal for me."

Mark winked at Andromeda in response. Audrey's eyes darted between Mark and Andromeda, and she nervously smiled.

"Well, I'm glad that's all done now," said Audrey, grabbing Mark by the sleeve. "Come, Mark, it's cold, and I will have to pee by the time we get back."

Andromeda looked on suspiciously as the two visitors left the house. She closed the door, and after a pause, looked down at Turd. "I wonder why he winked at me, and Audrey seemed to get nervous," Andromeda asked the puppy. "Do you suppose they suspect anything about John M.?"

"I have no clue," answered Turd. "But what I do know is that they are one interesting couple."

Andromeda sat down on the couch as Turd hopped up onto her lap. The two sat silently in the dim room, illuminated only by the light of the Christmas tree.

"This is nice," sighed Andromeda. "To be able to relax and just listen in the silence."

Turd farted.

"Ugh, Turd!" exclaimed Andromeda.

"What?" yelped the animal.

Andromeda chuckled. "Merry Christmas, Turd," she said, pushing the hair from her face and sighing.

"Merry Christmas . . . Doctor Andromeda Fallout," replied the puppy.

THE END

. . . or . . .

THE BEGINNING?